I Want to Be a
TRICERATOPS

by Thomas Kingsley Troupe

illustrated by Jomike Tejido

I practised my kickflips on the pavement as my little sister, Sarah, played with her toy dinosaurs.

"Raaar," Sarah growled, making her dinosaurs fight.

Then our older brother Jeremy and his friend Ben walked over. They kicked her toys down. "Now they're extinct!" Jeremy shouted. Ben laughed.

They made me so angry. "I want to be a
Triceratops," I whispered, heading towards
Sarah. "Then no one would mess with us!"

3

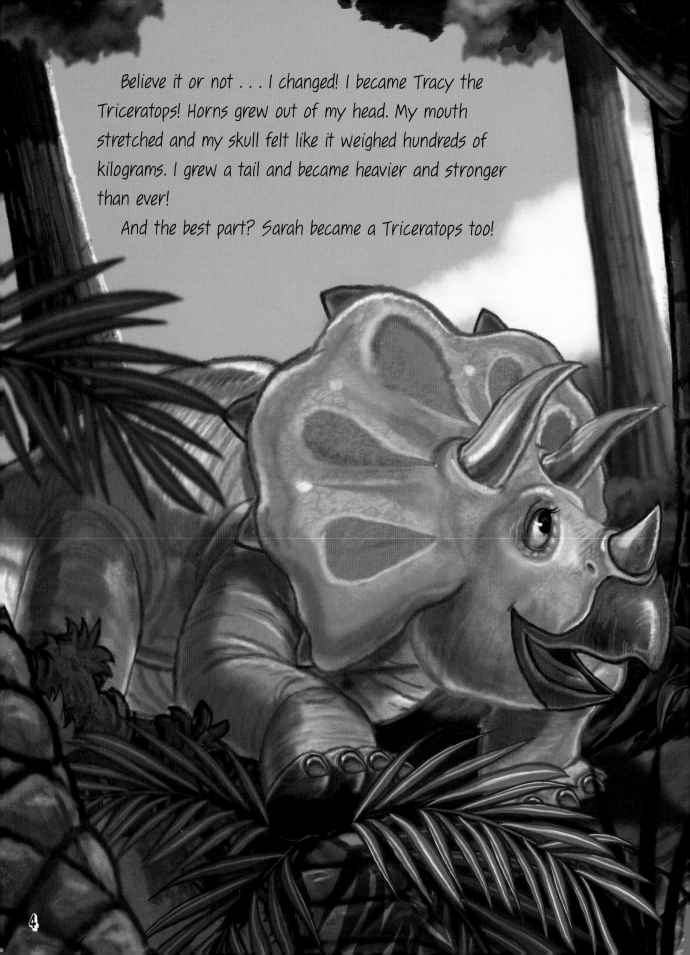

Believe it or not . . . I changed! I became Tracy the Triceratops! Horns grew out of my head. My mouth stretched and my skull felt like it weighed hundreds of kilograms. I grew a tail and became heavier and stronger than ever!

And the best part? Sarah became a Triceratops too!

"Where are we, Tracy?" Sarah asked.

"The past, I guess," I said.

The world around us looked totally different. Trees and bushes I'd never seen before were everywhere. Small lizards ran past us.

Another Triceratops peeked out from some bushes.

"Hey," he said. "I've never seen you two before. I'm Trey."

A LOOOONG TIME AGO . . . Triceratops lived during the end of the Cretaceous Period. This period lasted from 145 to 66 million years ago. Other animals that lived at that time included Gallimimus, Ankylosaurus and Tyrannosaurus rex.

We told Trey our names and followed him through the woods.
I couldn't get used to how heavy my head felt. It was like
carrying an armoured tank on my neck! Having a stubby tail felt
strange too. I could move it around. It brushed against trees
and bushes.

The horn above my nose was hard to get used to as well.
Anywhere I looked, I saw it!

"I need to get back to my family," Trey said. "They're in danger."

"Why?" I asked. "What's happening?"

The ground below my stubby feet trembled. Was it an earthquake? I stopped and Sarah looked scared.

"One by one, we're disappearing," Trey said. He hung his horned head in sadness.

The ground shook again. In the distance, I heard a loud, angry roar.

"We're being attacked," Trey said. "There's a hungry Tyrannosaurus rex on the loose. If we stick together, we've got a better chance of surviving."

I looked at Sarah's long, sharp horns. I couldn't imagine a big mouth like a T-rex wanting to eat us.

"Can we help?" I asked.

Trey led us toward the edge of the woods, then stopped us. "Don't move," he whispered.

We stopped in time to see a gigantic Tyrannosaurus rex attack. It snapped at a Triceratops with its awful teeth!

Sarah moved closer to me. "I don't want to get eaten," she whispered.

IT'S GREEK TO ME! The name Triceratops comes from three Greek words: tri (three), keras (horn) and ops (face). Together they mean "three-horned face."

9

"Let's go deeper into the woods," Trey said. "We should eat to keep up our strength."

I was a little hungry, but I didn't want to eat another dinosaur. Sarah and I watched as Trey bit into a big, thorny bush on the ground.

"Eat up," he said, with branches and leaves hanging out of his mouth.

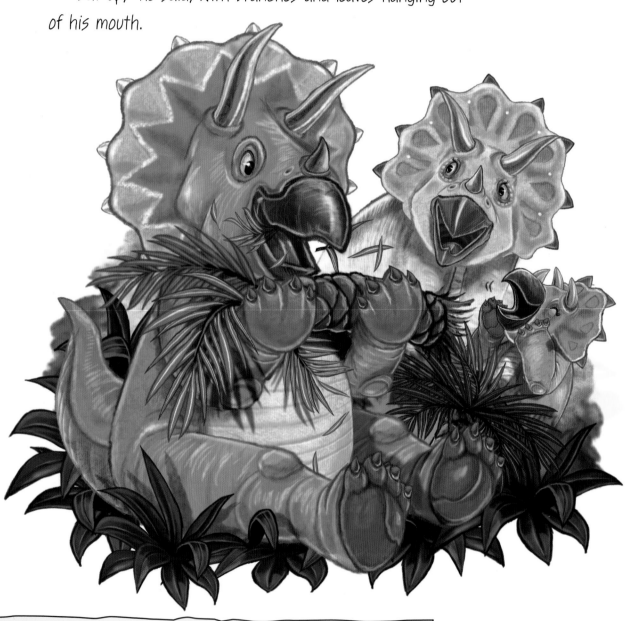

TEETH TO SPARE! A Triceratops could have as many as 800 teeth in its mouth. Any time a tooth fell out, another would rise up to take its place. Imagine flossing all of those teeth!

I tasted some leaves from a smaller plant nearby. They didn't taste too bad, but they were kind of chewy.

"Want the good stuff?" Trey asked. "Watch this." Using the horns on his head, he pushed against a tree until it fell over.

"The leaves on top taste best," he said. As Trey and Sarah ate, I kept my head up. I kept watching for that nasty big mouth, T-rex.

After eating and sneaking through the woods, we found Trey's family.

"What's that stink?" I asked, as Sarah and one of Trey's little brothers wandered off to play.

"Mum can't sit on her eggs to warm them up. She'd crush them!" Trey said. "Rotting plants help keep the eggs warm."

I saw half-buried eggs in the ground. The smelly, rotting plants formed a ring around them.

LEAVE MY BABIES ALONE! Many scientists think that Triceratops used its sharp horns to defend its young.

Suddenly, I heard a small voice call from the distance. "Tracy!"
I looked around, but couldn't find Sarah. Then I heard a roar.
I knew she was in trouble. I peeked through some thick bushes.
A T-rex stood roaring down into a deep gulch. Sarah and
Trey's brother were on a small ledge just below the edge of the
cliff. There was nowhere for the little ones to escape!

Since I couldn't run fast, I snuck up behind the T-rex. It made so much noise it couldn't hear me. When I was close enough, I rammed my horned head into its leg.

The T-rex roared in pain. I gave it a second nudge with my head. It tipped over and fell into the deep gulch. I heard it roar all the way down.

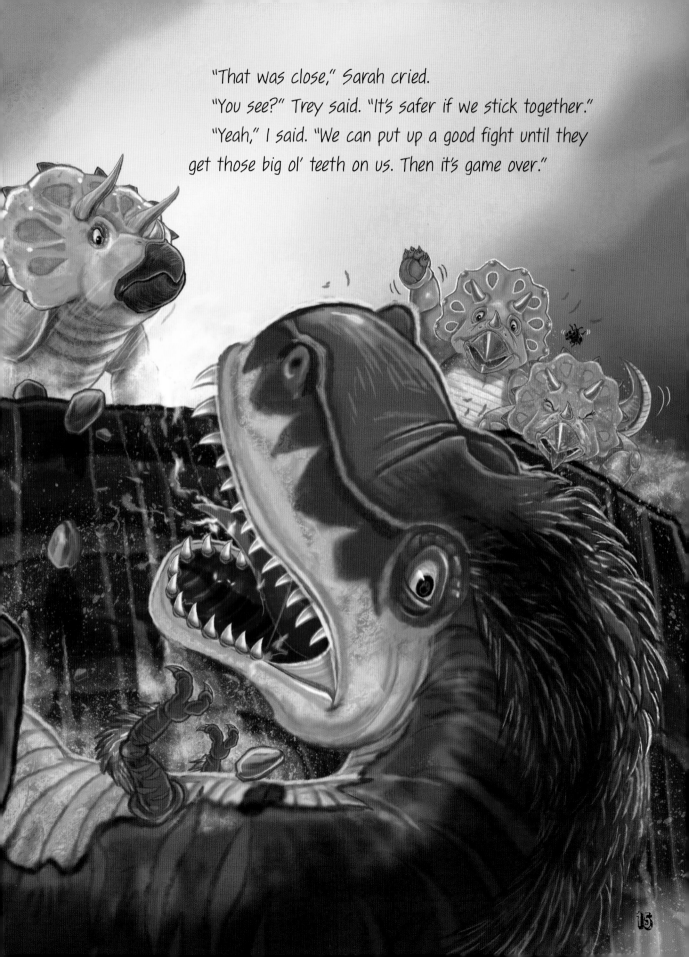

"That was close," Sarah cried.

"You see?" Trey said. "It's safer if we stick together."

"Yeah," I said. "We can put up a good fight until they get those big ol' teeth on us. Then it's game over."

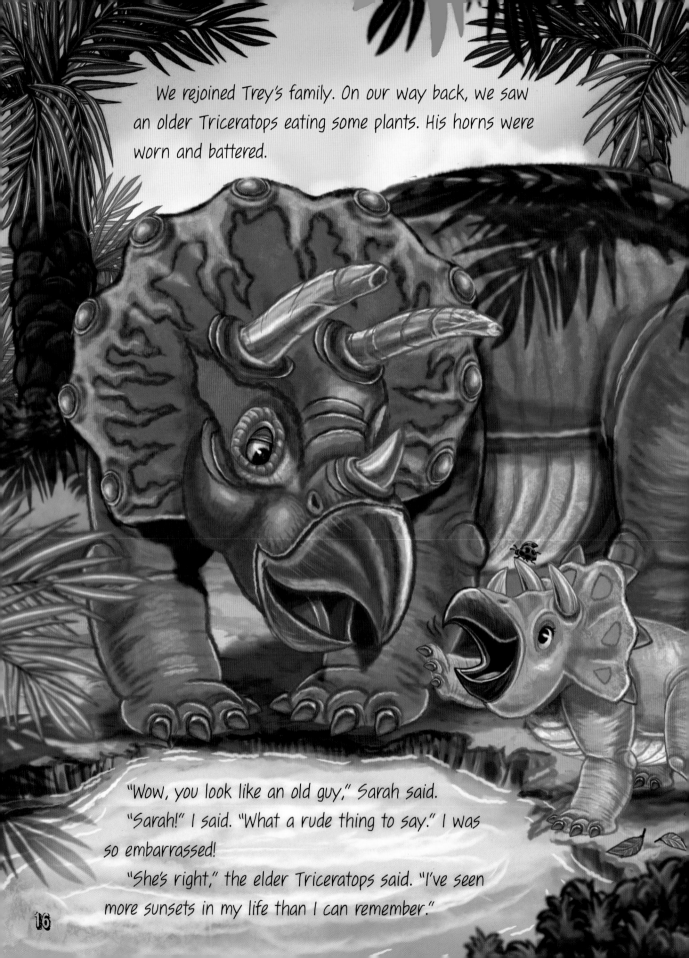

We rejoined Trey's family. On our way back, we saw an older Triceratops eating some plants. His horns were worn and battered.

"Wow, you look like an old guy," Sarah said.

"Sarah!" I said. "What a rude thing to say." I was so embarrassed!

"She's right," the elder Triceratops said. "I've seen more sunsets in my life than I can remember."

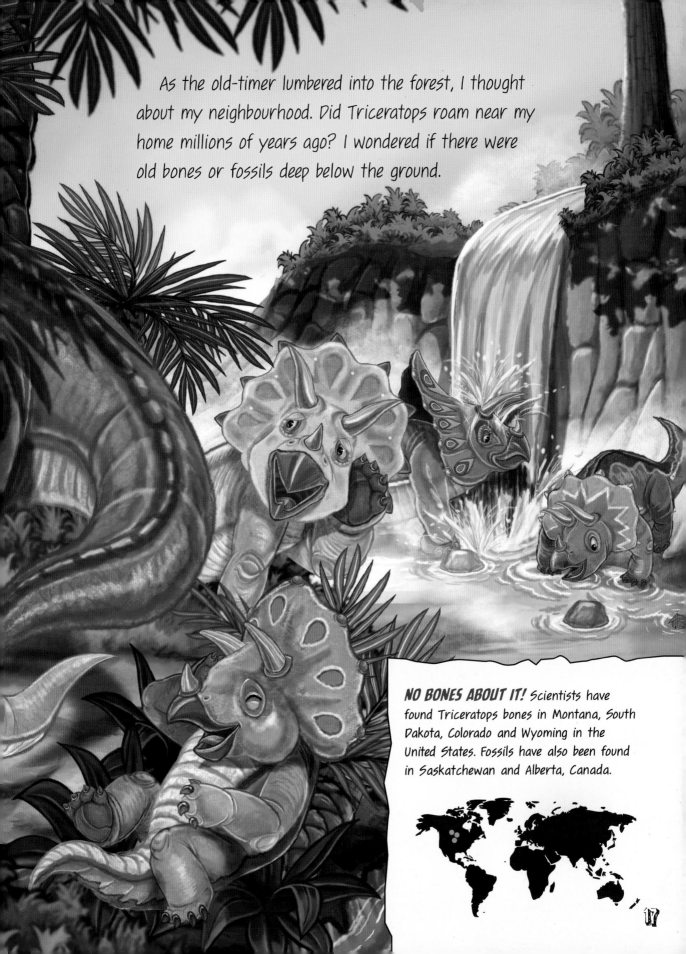

As the old-timer lumbered into the forest, I thought about my neighbourhood. Did Triceratops roam near my home millions of years ago? I wondered if there were old bones or fossils deep below the ground.

NO BONES ABOUT IT! Scientists have found Triceratops bones in Montana, South Dakota, Colorado and Wyoming in the United States. Fossils have also been found in Saskatchewan and Alberta, Canada.

As we wandered through the woods, the area around us began to change. The dinosaurs faded away. Trees disappeared and our apartment building was back. Before Sarah and I knew it, we were ourselves again.

Her toy dinosaurs were scattered around the front steps. I helped her gather them back up.

As we played with her Triceratops, Jeremy
and his friend came back again.

"Everyone knows the T-rex was the best
dinosaur," Jeremy shouted.

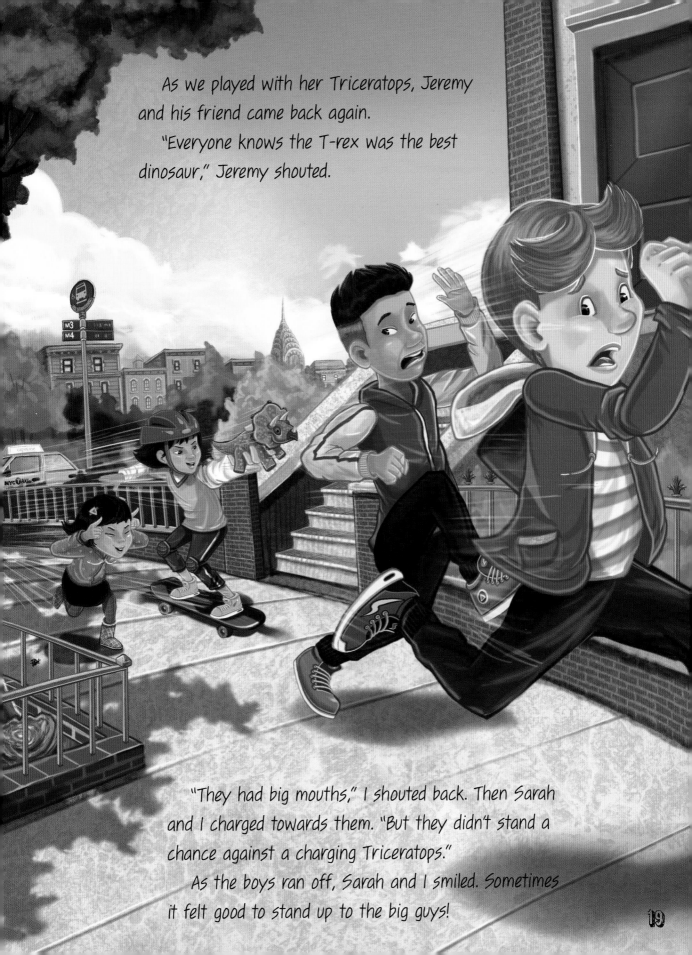

"They had big mouths," I shouted back. Then Sarah
and I charged towards them. "But they didn't stand a
chance against a charging Triceratops."

As the boys ran off, Sarah and I smiled. Sometimes
it felt good to stand up to the big guys!

MORE ABOUT TRICERATOPS

Triceratops is from the Ceratopsid family of dinosaurs. They were dinosaurs with horns on their heads, parrot-like beaks and neck frills. Other Ceratopsids include: Achelousaurus, Protoceratops, Centrosaurus and Styracosaurus.

Some scientists think a two-horned dinosaur named Nedoceratops was another species of Triceratops.

The largest Triceratops skull ever found was about 2.5 metres (8.2 feet) long. It was one of the largest known skulls among land animals at the time it was found.

Some scientists think that Triceratops may have had feathers all over its body. Little bumps on Triceratops' body might have been places where feathers or quills were once attached. An early relative to Triceratops, called Psittacosaurus, had a row of plumes running down the top of its tail.

Triceratops' head was so heavy the dinosaur most likely couldn't stand up on its hind legs. As a result, Triceratops was limited to eating low-growing bushes and plants.

Triceratops were among the last dinosaurs to exist before all dinosaurs (other than birds) became extinct at the end of the Cretaceous Period, 65 million years ago.

GLOSSARY

beak the hard front part of the mouth of birds and some dinosaurs; also called a bill

extinct no longer living; an extinct animal is one that has died out, with no more of its kind

frill a bony collar that fans out around an animal's neck

fossil the remains or traces of an animal or a plant, preserved as rock

gulch a deep valley that fills with water when it rains

herd a large group of animals that lives or moves together

life span the number of years a certain kind of plant or animal usually lives

quill the long, hollow central part of a bird's feather

species a group of animals with similar features

stubby thick and short in length

READ MORE

Armored Dinosaurs (Discovering Dinosaurs), Jinny Johnson (Black Rabbit Books, 2015)

Can you Tell a Triceratops from a Protoceratops? (Dinosaur Look-Alikes), Buffy Silverman (Lerner Publications Company, 2015)

Triceratops and Other Horned Dinosaurs: The Need-to-Know Facts (Dinosaur Fact Dig), Kathryn Clay (Capstone Press, 2016)

WEBSITES

www.nhm.ac.uk/discover/dino-directory/index.html
Explore the Natural History Museum's dino directory to see images, and learn facts and figures about your favourite dinosaurs.

www.youtube.com/watch?v=JBJjpJDzCBo&list=PLm12k9Kod2HQHrzitEDyyqSWi5ycfNVoM
Watch a fun video clip about Triceratops.

www.youtube.com/watch?v=mAm4wDNuZ38
Watch this animated video introduction to the incredible world of dinosaurs.

INDEX

defences 8, 12, 15

discovery 17, 20

eggs 12

extinction 21

food 10, 11, 21

fossils 17

horns 4, 6, 8, 9, 11, 12, 14, 16, 20

legs 21

nests 12

size 20, 21

tails 4, 6, 20

teeth 10

young 12, 13

BOOKS IN THE SERIES

Raintree is an imprint of Capstone Global Library Limited, a company incorporated in England and Wales having its registered office at 7 Pilgrim Street, London, EC4V 6LB – Registered company number: 6695582

www.raintree.co.uk
myorders@raintree.co.uk

Text © Capstone Global Library Limited 2017
The moral rights of the proprietor have been asserted.

Editors: Christopher Harbo and Anna Butzer
Designer: Sarah Bennett
Art Director: Ashlee Suker
Production Specialist: Kathy McColley

ISBN 978 1 4747 1482 2
20 19 18 17 16
10 9 8 7 6 5 4 3 2 1

British Library Cataloguing in Publication Data
A full catalogue record for this book is available from the British Library.

The illustrations in this book were planned with pencil on paper and finished with digital paints.

We would like to thank Mathew J. Wedel, PhD for his expertise, research and advice.

Every effort has been made to contact copyright holders of material reproduced in this book. Any omissions will be rectified in subsequent printings if notice is given to the publisher.

All the internet addresses (URLs) given in this book were valid at the time of going to press. However, due to the dynamic nature of the internet, some addresses may have changed, or sites may have changed or ceased to exist since publication. While the author and publisher regret any inconvenience this may cause readers, no responsibility for any such changes can be accepted by either the author or the publisher.

Printed and bound in China.